Welcome to ALADDIN QU

If you are looking for fast, f
with colorful characters, lots of kid-friendly
humor, easy-to-follow action, entertaining
story lines, and lively illustrations, then
ALADDIN QUIX is for you!

But wait, there's more!

If you're also looking for stories with
tables of contents; word lists; about-the-
book questions; 64, 80, or 96 pages; short
chapters; short paragraphs; and large fonts,
then **ALADDIN QUIX** is definitely for you!

ALADDIN QUIX: The next step between ready
to reads and longer, more challenging chapter
books, for readers five to eight years old.

Costume Parade

Read more ALADDIN QUIX books!

By Stephanie Calmenson

Our Principal Is a Frog!

Our Principal Is a Wolf!

Our Principal's in His Underwear!

Our Principal Breaks a Spell!

Our Principal's Wacky Wishes!

Our Principal Is a Spider!

Our Principal Is a Scaredy-Cat!

Our Principal Is a Noodlehead!

The Adventures of Allie and Amy
By Stephanie Calmenson and Joanna Cole

Book 1: *The Best Friend Plan*

Book 2: *Rockin' Rockets*

Book 3: *Stars of the Show*

The Adventures of
ALLIE and AMY
Costume Parade

By Stephanie Calmenson and Joanna Cole
Illustrated by James Burks

ALADDIN QUIX

New York   London   Toronto   Sydney   New Delhi

ALADDIN QUIX

Simon & Schuster Children's Publishing Division

1230 Avenue of the Americas, New York, New York 10020

First Aladdin QUIX paperback edition July 2022

Text copyright © 1999 by Joanna Cole and Stephanie Calmenson

Illustrations copyright © 2022 by James Burks

The text of this book was originally published

in slightly different form as *Gator Halloween* (1999).

Also available in an Aladdin QUIX hardcover edition.

All rights reserved, including the right of reproduction in whole or in part in any form.

ALADDIN and the related marks and colophon are

trademarks of Simon & Schuster, Inc.

For information about special discounts for bulk purchases, please contact

Simon & Schuster Special Sales at 1-866-506-1949 or business@simonandschuster.com.

The Simon & Schuster Speakers Bureau can bring authors to your live event. For

more information or to book an event contact the Simon & Schuster Speakers Bureau

at 1-866-248-3049 or visit our website at www.simonspeakers.com.

Designed by Heather Palisi

The illustrations for this book were rendered digitally.

The text of this book was set in Archer Medium.

Manufactured in the United States of America 0622 OFF

2 4 6 8 10 9 7 5 3 1

Library of Congress Control Number 2021945997

ISBN 9781534452602 (hc)

ISBN 9781534452596 (pbk)

ISBN 9781534452619 (ebook)

To Sloane Langer

Cast of Characters

Amy Cooper: Allie Anderson's best friend

Allie Anderson: Amy Cooper's best friend

Marvin Lopez: Dave Wang's buddy

Dave Wang: Marvin Lopez's buddy

Gracie Barnes: Bouncy, bubbly joke-telling neighbor and friend of Allie and Amy

Madame Lulu: Fortune-teller who is really Mrs. Suzie Tompkins, a neighbor in Allie's building

Louie: Lost lizard

Mr. Michael Angelo: Owner of Michael Angelo's Art Store

Contents

Costume Parade

1

Ring, Ring, Boo!

Ring! Ring! On Saturday morning the telephone rang at **Amy**'s house.

"I'll get it!" called Amy.

She was sure it was **Allie**. Allie Anderson and Amy Cooper were best friends. When they weren't together, they were talking on the phone.

"Hello," said Amy into the phone.

"Boo!" said a voice at the other end.

"Boo to you, Allie," said Amy.

"Allie whooo?" said the voice. "There's no Allie here. This is the ghost next door."

"Ooh, I'm scared," said Amy. "I'm shaking in my shoes."

"Well, I *could* have been a ghost,"

said the voice, which definitely was Allie's. "It's almost Halloween."

"**Eek!** We haven't thought about our costumes yet!" said Amy.

"Don't worry, we will," said Allie. "Meet me downstairs!"

"I'm on my way," said Amy.

Allie and Amy each lived on the sixth floor. Their buildings were right next door to each other.

Amy got into her elevator and pushed the first-floor button. Allie did the same thing in her elevator.

Both elevators went down: *Six, five, four, three, two, one!*
The girls **burst** out of their buildings at the exact same time.
"We need costumes that are

★ 4 ★

special—ones that no one else would think of," said Amy.

"We need a **genius** plan," said Allie.

"We should make costumes that go together," said Amy. "I know! We can be ketchup and mustard."

"**Ugh.** I hate mustard," said Allie. "How about a pencil and an eraser?"

"Erase that idea," said Amy. "We can do better."

"You're right," said Allie.

The girls had some thinking to do. While they were thinking—**whoosh!**—a skateboard whizzed by. On top of the skateboard was a boy named MARVIN.

Marvin could be fun sometimes. Other times, he could be very annoying.

Whoosh! A second skate-board whizzed by. It was carrying

DAVE.

Marvin and Dave were best buddies. Annoying times two!

The skateboards circled around and stopped in front of Allie and Amy.

"What are you two doing?" asked Marvin.

"We're thinking," said Amy.

"Is that why there's steam coming out of your ears?" said Dave.

"Don't even answer that," Allie said to Amy.

Just then **Gracie** came along. Gracie was their bouncy, bubbly neighbor.

"Hi, everyone!" she said, bouncing up and down. "I can't stop now. I'm going to my father's

house this week. I'll be back in time for the contest."

"What contest?" asked Amy and Allie at the same time.

"The costume contest. It's at Peabody Palace," said Gracie. "Speaking of Halloween, here's a spooky joke: What kind of gum do ghosts chew?"

Before they could answer, she called out, **"Boo-ble gum!"** Then she bounced off down the street.

After Gracie left, Allie, Amy,

Marvin, and Dave sat down. Now that they knew there was going to be a costume contest, they had some serious thinking to do.

2

What Costumes?

Suddenly Marvin stood up.

"I've got a great idea for my costume!" he said. "It will be so much fun when I win the prize."

"Or when *I* win it," said Dave. "I've got an idea too."

Marvin and Dave stepped aside and whispered their ideas to each other.

"We'll win the contest together!" said Marvin.

"Right!" said Dave.

Allie and Amy looked at each other. They were not going to take that bragging sitting down, so both jumped up at once.

"Excuse me," said Allie. "I must **inform** you that the prize is already taken. We are going to win the contest."

"The two of you can be the first to **congratulate** us," added Amy.

"Not a chance," said Marvin. "The two of *you* had better start practicing your speech. It will begin, 'Congratulations, Marv and Dave.'"

"No way," said Amy. "We're going to win because our costumes will be special—ones that no one else would think of."

"You just described our costumes exactly," said Dave.

"Oh, really? Well, we already

started making ours. You should see them," said Allie. "They're prizewinners. Isn't that right, Amy?"

Amy **hesitated** only a second.

"They sure are!" she said. **"They're the best ever!"**

"In your dreams," said Marvin. "*Ours* are the best."

"I think it's time to go now," said Allie. "We have to put the finishing touches on our costumes."

"On our *prizewinning* costumes!" said Amy.

The girls linked arms and stomped off with their noses in the air.

When they were a few feet away, Amy whispered to Allie, "What costumes? We have no idea what we're going to be, do we?"

"Not a clue," Allie whispered back. "Let's go you-know-where."

"To see you-know-who!" said Amy.

They turned the corner and raced to Madame Lulu's Fortune-Telling Parlor. They needed help—and fast!

3

Madame Lulu Says

Allie and Amy stood outside Madame Lulu's.

"When I count to three, we'll walk in together," said Allie.

At Madame Lulu's it felt like Halloween every day of the year.

The fortune-telling parlor was pink and yellow outside, but dark and spooky inside. The girls knew **Madame Lulu** was really their nice neighbor Mrs. Tompkins. But Allie and Amy were still always a little scared to go in.

"One, two, three!" counted Allie. Neither of them took a step.

Clink! The girls heard a familiar sound. Madame Lulu wore about twenty bracelets on each arm. They clinked together whenever she moved. Allie and Amy could see her shadow through the beaded curtain.

"Enter, fortune seekers! I've been waiting for you," called a **husky** voice.

Allie and Amy squeezed each other's hands as they walked

inside. Madame Lulu was dressed in black. A **veil** covered her head.

"What brings you here?" she asked, pointing to two chairs.

"W-w-we want our fortunes told, please," said Allie, sliding into one of the chairs.

"We need to know what Halloween costumes we'll wear and if we'll win the contest," said Amy, sliding into the other chair. "Can you help us?"

"Maybe," said the fortune-teller. She held out her hand. *Clink!*

Allie and Amy each dropped
a coin into her palm. She slipped
the coins into her pocket. **Clink!**
Clink! Then she gazed into her
crystal ball.

"I see darkness. It's darker than usual," she said. "In fact, I can hardly see a thing."

"Um . . . your veil is covering your eyes," said Allie.

Madame Lulu's veil had slipped down to her chin.

"Ah, yes, you're right," she said. She pushed back the veil. **Clink!**

"That's better," said Madame Lulu. "I see costumes. I see a parade!"

"Wow! It's the Halloween parade," said Amy. She turned

to Allie and whispered, **"She's amazing!"**

"Can you see us? Can you see what we're wearing?" asked Allie.

"It's crowded at the parade," said Madame Lulu.

"Our costumes go together. We're a pair," said Amy.

"Aha! I see a pair of socks!" said Madame Lulu.

"Eewww, smelly! That couldn't be us," said Amy. "Do you see anything else?"

Madame Lulu leaned over and **squinted** at her crystal ball.

"It's growing dark again," she said, holding out her hand. ***Clink!*** Allie and Amy dropped two more coins into Madame Lulu's palm.

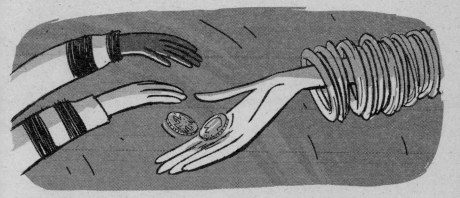

"Much better," said Madame Lulu. "Now I see a baseball and a bat."

"That wouldn't be us. We like soccer," said Allie.

"I see a cup and saucer," exclaimed Madame Lulu. "In fact, it's time for my coffee break."

Madame Lulu jumped up.

"But we don't know what our costumes will be!" said Allie.

"Don't worry, you have good ideas all the time. Take a chance! Try your luck! You'll think of something," called Madame Lulu as she headed for the back room.

"We have one last question— will we win the contest?" asked Amy.

"You girls are always winners!" called Madame Lulu over her shoulder.

The next thing they heard was

coffee pouring into a cup. Their visit was over. The girls walked out into bright sunshine.

"Madame Lulu said we're winners!" cried Amy. "This is so great!"

"Now all we have to do is figure out our costumes," said Allie. "Not a problem."

4

A Winning Idea

The girls headed to Amy's house for lunch. On the way they saw a sign that had a picture of a bright green lizard with orange spots. The sign said LOST! PLEASE FIND LOUIE.

"Ooh, he's so cute!" said Allie.

"I'll bet he's scared," said Amy.
"I got lost once, and it was awful."

"Let's try to find him on our
way home," said Allie.

They looked high and low. But
they didn't spot **Louie**.

"Maybe his owner found him
already," said Allie.

"I hope so," said Amy. "Otherwise Louie's all alone out there."

When they reached Amy's house, her parents had lunch ready for them.

"What are you girls doing this afternoon?" asked Amy's father.

"We're making Halloween costumes," said Allie. "Only, we can't decide what to be."

"We've been thinking and thinking," said Amy.

"Maybe you're thinking too hard," said Amy's mother. "Try

doing something else. An idea might pop up out of the blue."

"That could work," said Allie.

Right after lunch, Amy said, "Let's go play my new board game, Lucky Ducky."

The girls set up the game in Amy's room. They rolled the dice to see who'd go first. Amy got the higher number.

"You're lucky already," said Allie.

Amy rubbed the dice in her hands and blew on them.

"Come on, dice, get lucky twice," she said, and tossed them onto the board.

"Seven!" said Amy.

She moved seven spaces. The game board read: *Pick a card.*

Amy took a card from the pile. It said, *Take a chance. Roll the dice again.*

"Wow, do you notice something?" asked Amy. "The card says, 'Take a chance.' That's what Madame Lulu told us to do."

"And she said, 'Try your luck,'" said Allie. "Maybe she was telling us to be a pair of dice."

"That's it! She's a genius!" said Amy.

"So are we!" said Allie. "We figured it out!"

They gave each other a high five.

"Our costumes will be easy to make. We just need boxes that are the right size and paint," said Allie.

Amy's mother had just the boxes they needed in the closet. She helped the girls cut holes for their arms and heads, and then cut the flaps off the bottoms for their legs.

"Let's go to the art store for the paint," said Amy.

"I can't believe it!" said Allie. "We told Marvin and Dave our costumes were almost finished, and now they really are!"

Allie and Amy got onto the elevator. *Six, five, four, three, two, one!* They were on their way.

5

You'll Never Guess

In no time they were walking into Michael Angelo's Art Store. The lost lizard poster they'd seen before was hanging on the door.

"Let's remember to keep looking for Louie," said Allie.

They stepped up to the counter. "Hi, **Mr. Angelo**! We need some black and white paint, please," said Allie.

"We're making our Halloween costumes," said Amy.

"What are you going to be? Penguins?" asked Mr. Angelo.

"No. It's a surprise," said Allie. "You'll see on Halloween."

"Then I'll stop guessing and get the paint," said Mr. Angelo.

He disappeared into the back room.

"Mr. Angelo looks sad today, doesn't he?" asked Allie.

"He really does. I wonder what's wrong," said Amy.

Just then the door flew open. Marvin and Dave came in, carrying their skateboards. A moment later Mr. Angelo came back with black and white paint for Allie and Amy.

"Hi, Mr. Angelo," said Marvin. "We need to get red paint for our Halloween costumes."

"What are you going to be? Apples?" asked Mr. Angelo.

"No," said Dave. "It's a—"

"I know, it's a surprise," said Mr. Angelo. "I'll get your paint."

While the girls were looking around to see if they needed anything else, Marvin and Dave noticed the cans of black and white paint on the counter.

"What are you two going to be? **Dalmatians**?" asked Marvin.

"No," said Allie.

"Salt and pepper?" said Dave.

"No, you'll never guess our costumes," said Amy.

"You won't guess ours in a **gazillion** years," said Dave.

"We wouldn't spend a gazillionth
of a second thinking about it," said
Amy. When Mr. Angelo came back,
the girls paid for their paint.

"Bye, Mr. Angelo," they called on their way out.

"Bye-bye, zebras!" called Marvin.

"We are not going to be zebras," said Allie.

"So long, newspapers!" called Dave.

"We are not going to be newspapers, either," said Amy. "You might as well give up. You'll never guess."

And they closed the door behind them.

On the way home they made sure to look for Louie.

"Poor guy must be a lonely lizard by now," said Amy.

"Hmm, where would I hide if I were a lizard?" wondered Allie. "I know! I'd hide *under* something."

She walked along looking down. She saw plenty of ants, but no lizard.

"Hmm, where would I hide if *I* were a lizard?" wondered Amy. "I'd hide somewhere up high."

She walked along looking up.

She saw birds in the sky and squirrels in trees, but no lizard.

Amy was looking up while Allie was looking down and—*bam!*—they smashed into each other.

"No lizard," said Amy.

"No lizard," said Allie, rubbing her head.

"Let's try again later," said Amy.

The girls hurried back to Amy's house to work on their costumes.

6

We Can't Be Late

"First we have to paint the boxes white," said Allie.

That took no time at all.

"We'll have to wait for the boxes to dry before we put on the dots," said Amy. "What should we do while we wait?"

"**I know!**" said Allie. "If we're going to be dice, we should practice rolling."

"It will be hard to roll wearing our boxes. But we can do cart-wheels!" said Amy.

"Good thinking," said Allie. **"One, two, three, go!"**

They cartwheeled into the kitchen, where Amy's father was making popcorn.

"**Bravo!**" he said when they

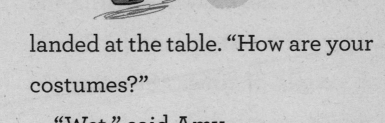

landed at the table. "How are your
costumes?"

"Wet," said Amy.

"Have some popcorn. It's dry," said her father. "It will be ready in a minute."

By the time the popcorn was eaten, the dice were ready for their spots. They each got twenty-one. The costumes were ready for Halloween, and so were Allie and Amy.

Over the next few days, Allie and Amy went out to look for Louie. A couple of times they thought they'd spotted him, but they hadn't. One false alarm turned out to be a bright green scarf. Another was a toy alligator.

Finally Halloween arrived.

Ding-dong! The doorbell rang at Amy's house.

"Trick-or-treaters already?" said Amy's mother, opening the door.

"No, it's me!" said Allie as she walked in, carrying her costume. "Amy and I have to hurry. We can't be late for the parade!"

The friends quickly put on their dice costumes. For finishing touches, Amy wore a white hair bow and white shoes. Allie wore a black hair bow and black shoes. They stood in front of the mirror. There were four dots on the front of Allie's costume and six dots on the front of Amy's.

"Four plus six equals . . . ," said Allie.

"A perfect ten!" said Amy. "That's us!"

"And we're going to win the contest!" said Allie. "Madame Lulu said so."

"That's right!" said Amy.

They headed out to Peabody Palace. They hadn't gone very far when they stopped short.

"Do you see what I see?" asked Allie, looking down a side street.

"You mean the bright green, **scaly** nose sticking out of that crack in the wall?" said Amy.

"Yes, it's Louie! Let's go get him," said Allie.

"Maybe we should come back for him later. We can't be late for the parade," said Amy.

"He might be gone by then," said Allie.

"You're right. We can't leave him. If he were my pet, I'd want someone to **rescue** him," said Amy. "Let's go!"

As soon as they got near, the nose disappeared farther into the wall.

"Uh-oh," said Amy. She ran and got a leaf. "Maybe he'd like something to eat," she said.

Amy **dangled** the leaf in front of the crack.

"He's not moving," said Allie. "Getting him out will take forever. We'll miss the contest."

"We've got to do something," said Amy. "He needs our help."

"Come out, Louie!" called Allie.

As soon as she called him, the lizard inched forward.

"Wow! He knows his name!" said Amy.

"Here, Louie!" called Allie and Amy together. **"Louie! Louie! Come out!"**

Inch by inch Louie crept out.

"One more baby lizard step, Louie," said Amy.

"He looks just like his picture," said Allie.

The girls **crouched** down, and Louie climbed onto Amy's head.

"I'm in love!" said Amy.

"I want him to climb on me!" said Allie.

Just then Louie took a giant leap and landed on Allie.

"Way to go, Louie!" said Allie.

"Uh-oh," said Amy, looking at her watch. "We *really* have to go now!"

"But what about Louie?" asked Allie.

"We'll bring him along," said Amy. "Louie, you're invited to a parade!"

7

Happy Halloween!

Louie had jumped back onto Amy.

"We're so lucky we found him," she said.

"And now we're going to win the contest," said Allie, gently patting Louie's tail.

The girls looked ahead. A witch with a tall black hat and a broom was standing on a platform, saying, "Congratulations to our second- and third-prize winners. And now for first prize. The winner is . . . the basketball!"

"Oh no!" said Amy. **"We missed the contest!"**

Everyone started to clap as the basketball bounced up to the platform.

"That's an especially bouncy basketball," said Allie.

"It's got to be Gracie," said Amy.

"Congratulations, you won!" said the witch. She handed a shiny jack-o'-lantern statue to the basketball. *Clink! Clink!*

"Did you hear those bracelets?" asked Allie.

"Madame Lulu is the witch!" said Amy.

They heard the basketball ask,

"Do you want to hear a Halloween joke?"

"That's *definitely* Gracie," said Amy.

"What do you call a Jack-o'-Lantern's sister?" asked the bouncy basketball. Without waiting for an answer, she called out, "Jill-o'-Lantern!"

"How can she be the winner?" asked Allie. "Madame Lulu said *we're* winners."

Clang! Clang! A red fire engine whizzed into view.

"We're here!" said the right side of the fire engine.

"You can give us our prize now," said the left side.

"Marvin? Dave? Is that you?" asked Allie.

"**Absolutely** not," said both sides together.

"Well, you're *absolutely* late," said Amy. "Gracie just won the contest."

Suddenly a voice called out from the crowd, **"Louie! It's my Louie!"**

Marvin's and Dave's heads popped up from the fire truck as everyone turned to see who the voice belonged to.

It was Mr. Angelo, who gently took the lizard from Amy's shoulder and hugged him.

"Louie, I missed you so much," he said.

"He's *your* pet lizard?" Amy asked Mr. Angelo.

"No wonder you looked so sad," said Allie.

Louie settled in happily on Mr. Angelo's shoulder.

"How did you find him? It couldn't have been easy," said Mr. Angelo.

"Well, it took a while. That's why we were late," said Allie.

"That means you missed the contest. For Louie. And for me," said Mr. Angelo.

"It was worth it," said Amy.

"I would like to reward you somehow," said Mr. Angelo. "If you had been in the contest, you might have won a prize. I know! How would you like drawing lessons?"

"**Wow!** That's a great prize, thank you," said Amy. "Louie can be our first **model**."

"Madame Lulu *said* we're winners!" said Allie.

"And she hasn't been wrong yet," said Amy.

The line was forming for the costume parade. Allie and Amy hurried to join.

★ ★ ★

Ding-dong! Later that night the doorbell rang at Madame Lulu's Fortune-Telling Parlor. The sun was going down, and it was starting to feel just a little bit spooky outside.

"Who is it?" called Madame Lulu from behind the beaded curtain.

She came outside and saw a pair of dice, a red fire engine, and a basketball.

"Trick or treat!" called five voices.

Madame Lulu dropped treats into everyone's Halloween bag.

"Don't go away," she said.

She brought out her crystal ball.

"Ooh, we're going to get our fortunes told!" said Allie.

"What do you see?" Marvin asked Madame Lulu.

"Do you see any tricks?" asked Amy.

Madame Lulu gazed into her ball.

"There will be no tricks for

you tonight," she said. "I see only treats in your future. **Happy Halloween!**"

The fire engine **clanged**. The basketball bounced. And the two lucky dice gave each other a high five, then cartwheeled happily down the street.

Word List

absolutely (ab·suh·LOOT·lee):
Totally, completely

burst (BERST): Sprang out
suddenly

clanged (KLANGD): Made a
loud, ringing, metal-like sound

congratulate
(kuhn·GRA·chuh·layt): To tell
someone you're glad they did
well

crouched (KROWCHD):
Lowered one's body by bending

the knees and getting close to
the ground

dalmatians (dal·MAY·shuns):
Medium-sized dogs that have short
white hair with many spots, which
are most often black or brown

dangled (DAYN·guld): Hung
loosely, allowing to swing freely

gazillion (guh·ZIL·yun): A huge
unstated number

genius (JEEN·yus): Very smart

hesitated (HEH·zuh·tay·ted):
Waited a bit before saying or
doing something

husky (HUH·skee): Sounding deep and rough

inform (in·FORM): To share knowledge with

model (MAH·duhl): A person or thing an artist uses as an example

rescue (REH·skyoo): To save from danger

scaly (SKAY·lee): Covered with small, flat, hard plates

squinted (SKWIN·ted): Looked with eyes partly closed

veil (VALE): A thin piece of cloth worn to cover one's face

Questions

1. If you and a friend wanted to make costumes that went well together, what would they be?

2. If you were a lost pet, where would you hide?

3. You have the chance to rescue a pet or get to an important place on time. Which would you choose to do?

4. How did Allie and Amy get to be winners, even when they didn't win the contest?

5. Lizards come in amazing color combinations. Can you draw a cool-looking lizard?

CHUCKLE YOUR WAY THROUGH THESE EASY-TO-READ ILLUSTRATED CHAPTER BOOKS!

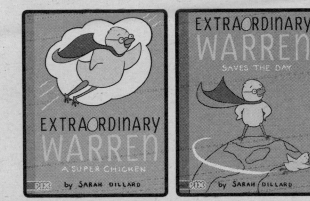

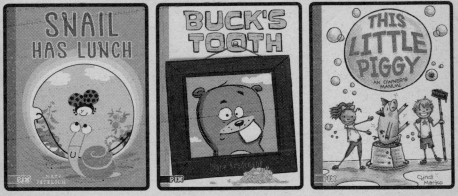

EBOOK EDITIONS ALSO AVAILABLE